Turtle's Race with Beaver

· A TRADITIONAL SENECA STORY ·

AS TOLD BY **Joseph Bruchac & James Bruchac**

PICTURES BY **Jose Aruego & Ariane Dewey**

PUFFIN BOOKS

PUFFIN BOOKS
Published by the Penguin Group
Penguin Young Readers Group, 345 Hudson Street,
New York, New York 10014, U.S.A.
Penguin Group (Canada), 10 Alcorn Avenue,
Toronto, Ontario, Canada M4V 3B2
(a division of Pearson Penguin Canada Inc.)
Penguin Books Ltd, 80 Strand, London WC2R 0RL, England
Penguin Ireland, 25 St Stephen's Green, Dublin 2, Ireland
(a division of Penguin Books Ltd)
Penguin Group (Australia), 250 Camberwell Road, Camberwell,
Victoria 3124, Australia (a division of Pearson Australia Group Pty Ltd)
Penguin Books India Pvt Ltd, 11 Community Centre, Panchsheel Park,
New Delhi - 110 017, India
Penguin Group (NZ), Cnr Airborne and Rosedale Roads, Albany, Auckland 1310,
New Zealand (a division of Pearson New Zealand Ltd)
Penguin Books (South Africa) (Pty) Ltd, 24 Sturdee Avenue, Rosebank, Johannesburg 2196, South Africa

Registered Offices: Penguin Books Ltd, 80 Strand, London WC2R 0RL, England

First published in the United States of America by Dial Books for Young Readers, a division of Penguin Young Readers Group, 2003
Published by Puffin Books, a division of Penguin Young Readers Group, 2005

20 19 18

THE LIBRARY OF CONGRESS HAS CATALOGED THE DIAL EDITION AS FOLLOWS:
Bruchac, Joseph, date.
Turtle's race with Beaver : a traditional Seneca story / as told by Joseph Bruchac and James Bruchac ; pictures by Jose Aruego and Ariane Dewey.   p.   cm.
Summary: When Beaver challenges Turtle to a swimming race for ownership of the pond, Turtle outsmarts Beaver, and Beaver learns to share.   ISBN 0-8037-2852-2
1. Seneca Indians—Folklore. 2. Tales—New York (State). [1. Seneca Indians—Folklore. 2. Indians of North America—New York (State)—Folklore. 3. Folklore—New York (State).]
I. Bruchac, James. II. Aruego, Jose, ill. III. Dewey, Ariane, ill. IV. Title.   E99.S3 B77 2003 398.2'089'9755—dc21   2002004001

Puffin Books ISBN 978-0-14-240466-9
Manufactured in China

The art for this book was prepared using pen-and-ink, gouache, and pastel. Designed by Nancy R. Leo-Kelly. Text set in Optima

To all good listeners,
both young and old

—*J.B. & J.B.*

To Juan

—*J.A. & A.D.*

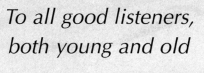

Authors' Note

For more than four decades, I've been learning from the oral traditions of our Northeastern Woodlands peoples, especially the Iroquois and Abenakis. I've heard many stories from more than one source, and this tale is no exception. One of the earliest written versions of "The Race of the Turtle and the Beaver" was published in 1923 in Arthur C. Parker's collection, *Seneca Myths and Folk Tales* (Buffalo Historical Society). It has been recorded in writing several times since.

However, this teaching tale is still very alive in the oral tradition. Among the Iroquois, where this particular story probably originates, I've heard it told in English by Seneca, Onondaga, and Mohawk storytellers. But I've also experienced versions of this story from the lips of Abenakis, Lenapes, and Penobscots. That's not surprising. The story of a weaker but wiser animal winning a race is one of the most common motifs in the animal tales of Native America.

In fact, such stories are found all around the world. Aesop's fable "The Tortoise and the Hare" is only one example. *Aesop,* by the way, means "Ethiopian," indicating that the ancient Greek slave who told that story was originally from Africa, where Tortoise and Hare stories are still told. My son Jim and I heard a similar tale from several storytellers in the West African country Mali during a 1992 visit.

Every storyteller brings something of himself or herself to the stories that become part of their repertoire. So it is that Jim, who first heard this tale from me thirty years ago and now shares it with others, does so in his own way. This co-authored telling is truly that. It reflects his voice and vision as much as it does my own.

—*Joseph Bruchac*

Over the years, I have shared our traditional tales with people of all ages. As a professional teacher and outdoor educator, I've found that stories about animals are by far my favorites. Our animal brothers and sisters are always teaching us things—in many ways. Of the stories I tell, those that involve interaction with the listeners are always the most fun to share. Like such tales as *How Chipmunk Got His Stripes,* this one not only contains important lessons but also brings the audience into the action.

—*James Bruchac*

Long ago, Turtle lived in a beautiful little pond.

She was very happy because this pond had everything a turtle needed. The water was just deep enough, there was plenty of food to eat, and there were lots of nice rocks just above the water for Turtle to sun herself on.

One day, as happens every year in the north, winter began to come to the land. As she had done year after year, Turtle swam to the bottom of the pond and buried herself in the thick mud.

While Turtle slept for the winter, another animal came walking along.
It was Beaver, who had been looking for a new home.
"This will be perfect," said Beaver, "once I make some changes."

Soon he began doing one of the things beavers do so well. *Chomp!*
Chomp! went Beaver as he took down one tree after another to build
a big dam.

He worked hard for many days. And as he did, the water got deeper and deeper.

After finishing his dam, Beaver made himself a fine lodge of mud and sticks, then settled in for the rest of the winter. He was very happy.

The moons came and went, and spring returned once more to the land. The birds sang and the ice melted away. Then Turtle woke up. Crawling out from under the mud, she began to swim toward the surface of the water. But she had to swim higher, and higher, and higher, and higher.

By the time Turtle made it to the surface, she realized that the water was four times as deep as before! Her pond didn't look the same at all. All of the rocks she loved to sun herself on were under water. On one side the pond stretched as far as her eyes could see. On the other stood a huge dam. Not too far from that was a big round lodge.

Then Turtle heard a loud *Whack!* She turned to see where the sound had come from. A strange animal was swimming toward her. It was Beaver.

"Who are you?" asked Beaver. "What are you doing here?"

"I am Turtle," Turtle said. "This is my pond. I have lived here my whole life."

"*Your* pond!" said Beaver. "This is *my* pond! Look at my wonderful dam and my splendid lodge. This is a beaver's pond."

"Yes," Turtle said, "I can see that you've done lots of work. Couldn't we just share the pond? There's plenty of room."

"Ha!" Beaver laughed. "I will not share my pond with any little turtle. But I *will* challenge you to a race. Whoever wins can stay, whoever loses must go find a new home."

Turtle didn't really want to race. She could see that Beaver, with his big flat tail, was probably a much faster swimmer. But this pond was the only home she knew.

"I agree," Turtle said. "We will race."

It was decided that the race would take place the next morning at first light. The two would meet on one side of the pond and race to the other. That night, Beaver told other animals about the race. Word began to spread throughout the forest.

Squirrel told Rabbit, Rabbit told Fox, Fox told Wolf, Wolf told Deer, Deer told Moose, Moose told Bear. Soon every animal in the forest knew.

Before first light came to the land, all of the animals of the forest gathered around the pond. As they waited for Turtle and Beaver to arrive, many chose sides. Most of the smaller animals, such as Mouse, Chipmunk, and Rabbit, sided with Turtle. Most of the bigger animals, such as Wolf, Moose, and Bear, sided with Beaver.

As they waited, they began to sing:

TURTLE! BEAVER! TURTLE! BEAVER! TURTLE! BEAVER!

They sang even louder when Beaver came swimming over from his lodge and Turtle popped up from under the water.

TURTLE! BEAVER! TURTLE!
BEAVER! TURTLE! BEAVER!

Turtle and Beaver took their positions on the shore.

Bear lifted his big paw in the air. "On your mark . . . get set . . . GO!"

SPLASH! went Beaver, leaping off from the shore. He was certain he would leave Turtle far behind. But Turtle had gotten an idea. Before Beaver hit the water, Turtle stretched out her long neck, opened her mouth, and bit into the end of Beaver's tail.

FLAP! FLAP! FLAP! went Beaver, swimming as fast as he could. But as fast as he went, Turtle was right behind, holding on as hard as she could.

The other animals kept cheering, but now some of the bigger animals were cheering for Turtle instead of Beaver.

TURTLE! BEAVER! TURTLE!
BEAVER! TURTLE! *TURTLE!*

Soon Beaver was halfway across the pond. Even though Turtle was still holding on, it looked as if Beaver would win for sure. Then Turtle bit a little harder into Beaver's tail.

FLAP! FLAP! FLAP! Beaver swam even faster. Turtle still held on. Now more of the animals were cheering for Turtle.

TURTLE! BEAVER! TURTLE!
TURTLE! TURTLE! TURTLE!

Now they were almost to the other side. Beaver seemed sure to win. But Turtle bit as hard as she could into Beaver's tail. *CRUNCH!*

"*YEEEE-OWWWW!*" yelled Beaver. He flipped his big flat tail up and out of the water. When his tail reached its highest point, Turtle let go.

"Weeee!" sang Turtle as she flew through the air right over Beaver's head.

KA-THUNK! Turtle landed on the far shore and crawled across the finish line. Turtle had won the race. All the animals cheered.

TURTLE! TURTLE! TURTLE!
TURTLE! TURTLE! TURTLE!

Turtle was very pleased. But she could see how sad Beaver was. "I would still be happy to share my pond," she said.

But Beaver was so embarrassed that he left without another word.

Over time Beaver's dam fell apart and the water got shallower and shallower. Turtle had back all her wonderful rocks to sun herself on.

As for Beaver, he did find a new home in a pond not too far away. In that pond, though, there also lived a turtle.

"Can I share your pond with you?" Beaver asked.

"Of course," that other turtle said.

And so the two of them lived there happily through all the seasons to come.